Rabbids at the Museum

Adapted by Cordelia Evans
Based on the screenplay written by Candice Corbeel
Illustrated by Jim Durk

Ready-to-Read

Simon Spotlight
New York   London   Toronto   Sydney   New Delhi

SIMON SPOTLIGHT
An imprint of Simon & Schuster Children's Publishing Division
1230 Avenue of the Americas, New York, New York 10020
This Simon Spotlight edition September 2015
SIMON SPOTLIGHT, READY-TO-READ, and colophon are registered trademarks of Simon & Schuster, Inc.
For information about special discounts for bulk purchases, please contact Simon & Schuster Special Sales at
1-866-506-1949 or business@simonandschuster.com.
Manufactured in the United States of America 0815 LAK
2 4 6 8 10 9 7 5 3 1
ISBN 978-1-4814-4111-7 (hc)
ISBN 978-1-4814-4110-0 (pbk)
ISBN 978-1-4814-4112-4 (eBook)

CONTENTS

CHAPTER 1:
The Masterpiece

A museum security guard carefully brushed a tiny speck of dirt off a pedestal displaying a crooked wheel—er, a very important piece of art.

When a fly buzzed a little too close, he quickly caught it with his bare hands.

Then he returned to his guard chair . . .

... where he promptly fell asleep.

Across the room, the museum's curator was sharing a new painting with an art dealer.

"And this is one of the abstract masterpieces of our collection," said the curator.

"Oh yes," said the art dealer, nodding. "This painting is obviously an attack against consumer society."

"I think my client will have a lot of great things to say about this collection," continued the art dealer.

"Bravo," the curator said. "Now, let me show you some of the other highlights of our collection." He led the dealer into another room of the museum.

The curator and the art dealer hadn't noticed another curious patron of the arts: a Rabbid. But after they left, the Rabbid revealed his own opinions about the painting.

"Bwah bwah bwah, bwah bwah, bwah bwah bwah bwah, bwah, bwah bwah bwah bwah BWAH," the Rabbid said.

CHAPTER 2:
The Thick Black Line

This Rabbid wasn't the only Rabbid visiting the museum today, however. A second Rabbid was also feeling artsy, but he wasn't just looking at the art—he was creating his own.

With a big black marker the Rabbid drew
a thick line across the floor of the museum.
He was concentrating so hard on his
artwork that he bumped right into the
security guard!

But the guard didn't wake up. . . . He just
let out an extra-loud snore.

The Rabbid continued happily drawing
his line. Well, to you it might look like
a line. To the Rabbid, it was probably a
masterpiece. Or maybe he just liked the
squeaky sound the marker made on
the floor.

Just then, the first Rabbid noticed that
the second Rabbid was drawing on the
floor. He immediately ran over and tried to
get his friend's attention. But the second
Rabbid was taking his art very seriously
and was not interested in hanging out at the
moment.

The first Rabbid started to get frustrated. He wanted a turn with the stick that made a line on the floor! He jumped up and down in front of the other Rabbid and made a lot of noise, but the second Rabbid just whispered, "Bwah bwah bwah," and pointed to the sleeping guard, who continued to snore away.

The drawing Rabbid continued his line across the room.

"BWAH!" shrieked the first Rabbid. The second Rabbid still ignored him, and the guard still snored . . . but he heard something else.

Bwah! Bwah! Bwah!

The Rabbid stopped, fascinated. He looked around. Were there other Rabbids in the museum, too? Did they have sticks that made lines on the floor?

What the Rabbid was hearing was an echo, but he didn't know that. What he did know was that if he made a very loud noise very close to someone's ear, and then the noise was repeated over and over, it might make that someone pay attention to him. . . .

CHAPTER 3:
Getting Squiggly

The Rabbid quietly snuck over to where the other Rabbid was still drawing on the floor (well, as quietly as a Rabbid can—he was still whispering, "Bwah bwah bwah!" to himself kind of loudly). When he was right behind the drawing Rabbid, he shouted, "Bwah!" again.

Sure enough, the other Rabbid jumped high in the air, and then covered his ears as the "Bwah!" echoed throughout the museum. The first Rabbid laughed and pointed. He turned around and shook his butt like a chicken, and said, "Bwok bwok bwok!" It's impossible to say why he did that, but it's possible he had forgotten that moments earlier he too had been afraid of the echo.

After the drawing Rabbid recovered from the shock of the echo, he looked down and noticed that his line now ended in a big squiggle! (The line wasn't straight in the first place, so it's unclear why the Rabbid was so upset that it was now squiggly— it must not have been part of his artistic vision.)

He screeched angrily at the other Rabbid. The Rabbid without the marker stuck his tongue out at the artist Rabbid and left in a huff.

The drawing Rabbid got back to work and continued his line, but he didn't get very far before he looked up and noticed the painting the other Rabbid had admired earlier.

The Rabbid was amazed. It looked just like his masterpiece, except it was on the wall, not the floor!

The Rabbid looked up at the painting, where the thick black line ran off the edge of the canvas. Then he looked down at the floor, where his thick black line ended.

He looked back up at the painting. Then back down at the floor.

Can you guess what the Rabbid was thinking?

CHAPTER 4:
Across the Force Field

If you guessed that the Rabbid wanted to connect his line to the line in the painting, you're right! The Rabbid set to work doing this, but he soon reached a white line that was even thicker than his black line.

This was just the white line that tells people at a museum when they're too close to a painting, but the Rabbid didn't know that, of course. He thought it was some sort of force field. And he had to figure out how to cross it.

First he tapped on the line with his foot. Nothing happened.

Then he stuck his tongue across the line. Nothing happened.

Finally he closed his eyes, put the marker in his mouth, and stretched his whole body across the line. Nothing happened. So he opened his eyes and stepped quickly across the line.

The Rabbid was so happy to make it
across the line that he did a little dance.
But, as usual, his dance moves were a
bit wild, and he knocked his marker back
across the line!

For some reason the Rabbid didn't realize that he could just walk back across the line and pick up his marker. Instead, his plan was to suck the marker in with his breath. Of course, he sucked in a little too much . . . and he ended up swallowing the marker.

Luckily, this Rabbid was very used to
eating things he wasn't supposed to, so
he reached into his mouth and pulled
the marker right out. He turned to
finally connect the two lines, but he was
interrupted again—this time, by a marker
cap that hit him on the head.

The first Rabbid was back with a marker
of his own!

CHAPTER 5:
On Guard!

The artist Rabbid groaned and tried to
ignore his fellow Rabbid. He went to draw
his line, but the other Rabbid was across
the room in a flash, blocking the drawing
Rabbid's marker with his own.

Soon it was a full-fledged swordfight—er,
marker fight.

The one Rabbid danced on the bench as the other Rabbid tried to draw on him with the marker. His dancing got a little too energetic, though, and when he went to spin on his head, the artist Rabbid was able to mark him!

The two Rabbids continued to fight,
and they started to get creative with their
marker attacks.

They kept fighting and drawing, running past the security guard, who was still sleeping. Soon they were both completely covered in marker.

Using a classic fighting technique, one Rabbid tripped the other, and they both went flying into the wall with the line painting, which slid down and fell face-first onto the two Rabbids.

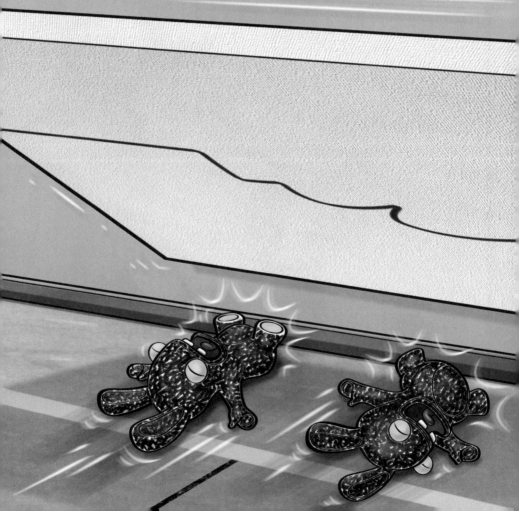

The two Rabbids crawled out from under the giant painting and lifted it back up against the wall. They noticed that it looked a little . . . different.

They definitely thought it was an improvement!

CHAPTER 6:
Call Security!

At this point, the security guard (who must have been very tired) finally woke up. He rushed across the room and grabbed both Rabbids by the ears.

"Hey, you two!" he shouted. "What are you doing in here? Why I ought to turn you into a—"

He was putting his face a little too close to one of the Rabbids. The Rabbid, whose arms were still free, thought the security guard could use some artwork on his face, too.

Another chase ensued, but this time, the two fighting Rabbids banded together against the security guard. They hid under a bench, which he flipped over. They jumped onto an art display, which he knocked over. They danced near a wall, which he drew on with the marker.

Soon the "Get back here!"s and the "Bwah
ha ha!"s (because the Rabbids thought this
was quite funny, obviously) got so loud that
the museum curator came back into the room.

"What is going—" he started to say, but
stopped when he saw what had happened.

Everyone was silent for a minute. The security guard looked at the marker in his hand, then swiftly hid it behind his back. One last painting that remained on the wall slid off and fell to the floor with a loud *smack!*

"You were drawing? On the *paintings?*" the curator shouted at the security guard. "Are you completely insane?"

"It was them!" said the guard, pointing at the Rabbids, who were hiding among the art. The Rabbids didn't flinch, and the curator turned back to the guard.

"You had better have this mess cleaned up in a flash, or you'll be guarding the toilets!"

The curator dragged the guard out of the room. The art dealer followed, but stopped to examine a piece of art she hadn't seen before.

"Now *that* is a masterpiece," she said.

The Rabbids waited until everyone had left the room, then climbed down off the power drill, laughing. They were still laughing when they turned the corner into the next room and saw another piece of artwork they felt they could improve. . . .